A is for Absent . . .

"Come on!" Dink dragged his friends down the street to the Book Nook.

They looked through the window, out of breath. The bookstore was crowded with kids. The Book Nook's owner, Mr. Paskey, had set up folding chairs. Dink noticed that most of them were already taken.

Dink saw Mr. Paskey sitting behind a table. A big white sign on the table said WELCOME, WALLIS WALLACE!

But the chair behind the sign was empty. Dink gulped and stared at the empty seat.

Where was Wallis Wallace?

This book is dedicated to Lori Haskins.
—R.R.

To Kathie, Jesse, and Molly
—J.S.G.

Text copyright © 1997 by Ron Roy
Cover art copyright © 2015 by Stephen Gilpin
Interior illustrations copyright © 1997 by John Steven Gurney

All rights reserved. Published in the United States by Random House Children's Books, a division of Random House LLC, a Penguin Random House Company, New York. Originally published in paperback by Random House Children's Books, New York, in 1997.

Random House and the colophon and A to Z Mysteries are registered trademarks and A Stepping Stone Book and the colophon and the A to Z Mysteries colophon are trademarks of Random House LLC.

Visit us on the Web!
SteppingStonesBooks.com
randomhousekids.com

Educators and librarians, for a variety of teaching tools, visit us at RHTeachersLibrarians.com

Library of Congress Cataloging-in-Publication Data
Roy, Ron.
The absent author / by Ron Roy ; illustrated by John Steven Gurney.
p. cm. — (A to Z mysteries)
"A Stepping Stone book."
Summary: Dink Duncan and his two friends investigate the apparent kidnapping of famous mystery author Wallis Wallace.
ISBN 978-0-679-88168-1 (trade) — ISBN 978-0-679-98168-8 (lib. bdg.) —
ISBN 978-0-307-51012-9 (ebook)
[1. Mystery and detective stories.] I. Gurney, John, ill. II. Title. III. Series: Roy, Ron. A to Z mysteries.
PZ7.R8139 Ab 1997 [Fic]—dc21 97-2030

Printed in the United States of America
60

This book has been officially leveled by using the F&P Text Level Gradient™ Leveling System.

A to Z Mysteries®

The Absent Author

by **Ron Roy**

illustrated by
John Steven Gurney

A STEPPING STONE BOOK™

Random House 🏠 New York

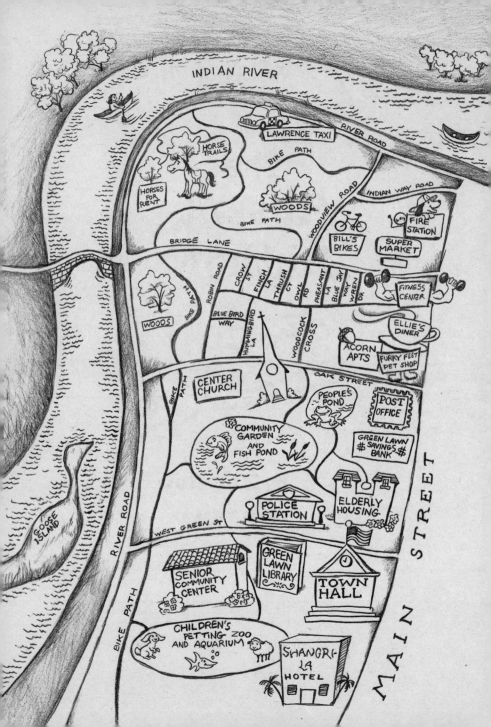

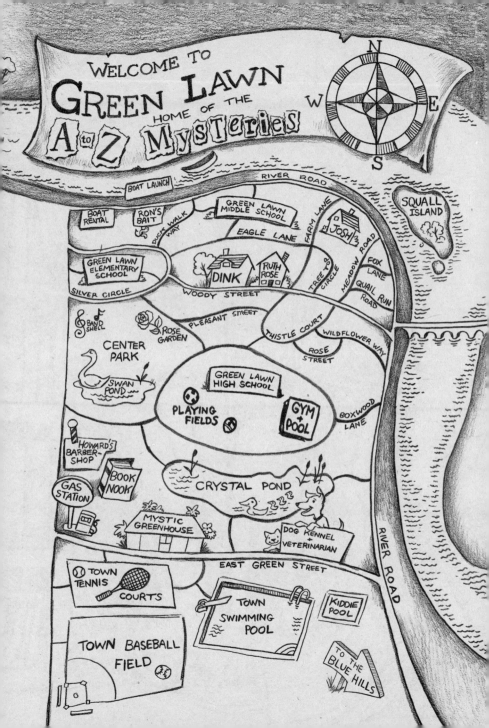

Chapter 1

"Please, Josh," Dink said. "If you come with me today, I'll owe you one. Just name it. *Anything!*"

Dink's full name was Donald David Duncan. But no one in Green Lawn ever called him that. Except his mother, when she meant business.

Josh Pinto grinned at his best friend.

"Anything?" He raised his mischievous green eyes toward the ceiling of Dink's bedroom. "Let's see, what do you have that I want?" He scratched his head. "I know, I'll take Loretta!"

Dink tossed a pillow at Josh. "When I said *anything,* I meant anything but my guinea pig! Are you coming with me or not? I have to be at the Book Nook in fifteen minutes!"

Dink rushed into the bathroom, tucking his shirt into his jeans at the same time. Josh followed him.

Standing in front of the mirror, Dink yanked a brush through his thick blond hair. "Well?" he asked. "Are you coming with me?"

"What's so important about this writer guy?" Josh asked, sitting on the edge of the bathtub.

Dink turned around and pointed his hairbrush. "Wallis Wallace isn't just some writer guy, Josh. He's the most famous mystery writer in the world! All the kids read his books. Except for you."

"If he's so famous, why's he coming to dinky little Green Lawn?"

Dink charged back into his bedroom. "I told you! He's coming because I *invited* him. I'm scared to death to meet someone so famous. I don't even know what you're supposed to say to an author!"

Dink dived under his bed and backed out again with his sneakers. "Please come with me?"

Josh leaned in the bedroom doorway. "Sure I'll come, you dope. I'm just trying to make you sweat. Usually you're so calm!"

Dink stared at his friend. "You will? Thanks! I can't believe Wallis Wallace is really coming. When I wrote and asked him, I never thought he'd say yes."

Dink yanked his backpack out of his closet. "Pack my books, okay? I'm getting Wallis Wallace to sign them all!"

Josh began pulling Wallis Wallace books off Dink's bookshelf. "Geez, how many do you have?"

"Every one he's written." Dink sat on the floor to tie his sneakers. "Twenty-three so far. You should read some of them, Josh."

Josh picked out *The Poisoned Pond* and read the back cover. "Hey, cool! It says here that Wallis Wallace lives in a castle in Maine! Wouldn't that be neat?"

Dink grinned. "When I'm a famous writer, you can live in my castle, Josh."

"No way. When I'm a famous *artist*, you can live in *my* castle. Down in the basement!"

Josh picked up *The Riddle in the River.* "What's this guy look like?" he asked. "And how come his picture isn't on any of these books?"

"I wondered about that, too," Dink said. "I sent him one of my school pictures and asked for one of him. But when I got his letter, there was no picture."

He finished tying his laces. "Maybe Wallis Wallace just doesn't like having his picture taken."

Josh squeezed all twenty-three books into Dink's pack. He grinned at Dink. "Or maybe he's just too ugly."

Dink laughed. "Gee, Josh, *you're* ugly and you love having your picture taken."

"Haw, haw." Josh picked up his drawing pad. "But just because you're my best friend, I'll draw his picture at the bookstore."

Dink looked at his watch. "Yikes!" he said. "We have to pick up Ruth Rose

in one minute!" He tore into the bathroom and started brushing his teeth.

"How'd you get her to come?" Josh
called.

Dink rushed back into his room,
wiping toothpaste from his mouth.
"You kidding? Ruth Rose loves Wallis
Wallace's books."

Dink slung his backpack over his
shoulder. He and Josh hurried next
door to 24 Woody Street. Tiger, Ruth
Rose's orange cat, was sitting in the sun
on the steps.

Dink pressed the doorbell.

Ruth Rose showed up at the door.

As usual, she was dressed all in one
color. Today it was purple. She wore
purple coveralls over a purple shirt and
had on purple running shoes. A purple
baseball cap kept her black curls out of
her face.

"Hey," she said. Then she turned

around and screamed into the house. "THE GUYS ARE HERE, MOM. I'M LEAVING!"

Dink and Josh covered their ears.

"Geez, Ruth Rose," Josh said. "I don't know what's louder, your outfit or your voice."

Ruth Rose smiled sweetly at Josh.

"I can't wait until Wallis Wallace signs my book!" she said. She held up a copy of *The Phantom in the Pharmacy*.

"I wonder if Wallis Wallace will read from the new book he's working on," Dink said.

"What's the title?" Ruth Rose asked.

They headed toward the Book Nook.

"I don't know," said Dink. "But he wrote in his letter that he's doing some of the research while he's here in Connecticut."

Dink pulled the letter out of his

pocket. He read it out loud while he walked.

Dear Mr. Duncan,

Thank you for your kind letter. I'm so impressed that you've read all my books! I have good news. I've made arrangements to come to the Book Nook to sign books. I can use part of my time for research. Thanks for your picture. I'm so happy to finally meet one of my most loyal fans. Short of being kidnapped, nothing will stop me from coming!

See you soon,

Wallis Wallace

The letter was signed *Wallis Wallace* in loopy letters. Dink grinned. "Pretty neat, huh?"

"Pretty neat, *Mister* Duncan!" teased Josh.

"You should have that letter framed," Ruth Rose said.

"Great idea!" Dink said.

They passed Howard's Barbershop. Howard waved through his window as they hurried by.

"Come on!" Dink urged as he dragged his friends down the street to the Book Nook.

They looked through the window, out of breath. The bookstore was crowded with kids. The Book Nook's owner, Mr. Paskey, had set up folding chairs. Dink noticed that most of them were already taken.

Dink saw Mr. Paskey sitting behind a table. A big white sign on the table said WELCOME, WALLIS WALLACE!

But the chair behind the sign was empty. Dink gulped and stared at the empty seat.

Where was Wallis Wallace?

Chapter 2

Dink raced into the Book Nook. Josh and Ruth Rose were right behind him. They found three seats behind Tommy Tomko and Eddie Carini.

Dink plopped his pack on the floor. The clock over the cash register said three minutes after eleven.

"Where is he?" Dink whispered to Tommy Tomko.

Tommy turned around. "Beats me. He's not here yet, and Mr. Paskey looks worried."

"What's going on?" Ruth Rose said.

Dink told her and Josh what Tommy had said.

"Paskey does look pretty nervous," Josh whispered.

"Mr. Paskey always looks nervous," Dink whispered back, looking around the room. He saw about thirty kids he knew. Mrs. Davis, Dink's neighbor, was looking at gardening books.

Dink checked out the other grownups in the store. None of them looked like a famous mystery writer.

Mr. Paskey stood up. "Boys and girls, welcome to the Book Nook! Wallis Wallace should be here any second. How many of you have books to be autographed?"

Everyone waved a book in the air.

"Wonderful! I'm sure Wallis Wallace will be happy to know that Green Lawn is a reading town!"

The kids clapped and cheered.

Dink glanced at the clock. Five past eleven. He swallowed, trying to stay calm. Wallis Wallace was late, but it was only by five minutes.

Slowly, five more minutes passed. Dink felt his palms getting damp. *Where* is *Wallis Wallace?* he wondered.

Some of the kids started getting restless. Dink heard one kid say, "Whenever *I'm* late, I get grounded!"

"So where is he?" Josh asked.

Ruth Rose looked at her watch. "It's only ten after," she said. "Famous people are always late."

Now Dink stared at the clock. The big hand jerked forward, paused, then wobbled forward again.

At 11:15, Mr. Paskey stood up again. "I don't understand why Wallis Wallace is late," he said. Dink noticed that his bald head was shiny with sweat. His bow tie was getting a workout.

Mr. Paskey smiled bravely, but his eyes were blinking like crazy through his thick glasses. "Shall we give him a few more minutes?"

The crowd grumbled, but nobody wanted to go anywhere.

Ruth Rose started to read her book.
Josh opened his sketch pad and
began drawing Mr. Paskey. Dink turned
and stared at the door. He mentally
ordered Wallis Wallace to walk through
it. *You have to come!* thought Dink.

Ever since he had received Wallis Wallace's letter, he'd thought about only one thing: meeting him today.

Suddenly Dink felt his heart skip a beat. THE LETTER! *Short of being kidnapped,* the letter said, *nothing will stop me from coming.*

Kidnapped! Dink shook himself. Of course Wallis Wallace hadn't been kidnapped!

Mr. Paskey stood again, but this time he wasn't smiling. "I'm sorry, kids," he said. "But Wallis Wallace doesn't seem to be coming after all."

The kids groaned. They got up, scraping chairs and bumping knees. Mr. Paskey apologized to them as they crowded past, heading for the door.

"I've read every single one of his books," Dink heard Amy Flower tell another girl. "Now I'll probably *never* meet anyone famous!"

"I can't believe we gave up a soccer game for this!" Tommy Tomko muttered to Eddie Carini on their way out.

Ruth Rose and Josh went next, but Dink remained in his seat. He was too stunned to move.

He felt the letter through his jeans. *Short of being kidnapped...* Finally Dink got up and walked out.

Josh and Ruth Rose were waiting for him.

"What's the matter?" Ruth Rose said. "You look sick!"

"I *am* sick," Dink mumbled. "I invited him here. It's all my fault."

"What's all your fault?" Josh asked.

"This!" he said, thrusting the letter into Josh's hands. "Wallis Wallace has been *kidnapped!*"

Chapter 3

"KIDNAPPED?" Ruth Rose shrieked. Her blue eyes were huge.

Josh and Dink covered their ears.

"Shh!" said Josh. He handed the letter back to Dink and gave a quick gesture with his head. "Some strange woman is watching us!"

Dink had noticed the woman earlier. She'd been sitting in the back of the Book Nook.

"She's coming over here!" Ruth Rose said.

The woman had brown hair up in a neat bun. Half-glasses perched on her nose. She was wearing a brown dress and brown shoes, and carried a book bag with a picture of a moose on the side. Around her neck she wore a red scarf covered with tiny black letters.

"Excuse me," she said in a soft, trembly voice. "Did you say Wallis Wallace has been *kidnapped?*" The woman poked her glasses nervously.

Dink wasn't sure what to say. He *thought* Wallis Wallace had been kidnapped, but he couldn't be sure. Finally he said, "Well, he might have been."

"My goodness!" gasped the woman.

"Who are you?" Josh asked her.

"Oh, pardon me!" The woman blushed. "My name is Mavis Green," she mumbled. "I'm a writer, and I came to meet Mr. Wallace."

Dink said, "I'm Dink Duncan. These are my friends Ruth Rose and Josh."

Mavis shook hands shyly.

Then she reached into her book bag and pulled out a folded paper.

"Wallis Wallace wrote to me last week. He said something very peculiar in his letter. I didn't think much of it at the time. But when he didn't show up today, and then I heard you mention kidnapping..."

She handed the letter to Dink. Josh and Ruth Rose read it over his shoulder.

Dear Mavis,

    Thanks for your note. I'm well, and thank you for asking. But lately my imagination is playing tricks on me. I keep thinking I'm being followed! Maybe that's what happens to mystery writers—we start seeing bad guys in the shadows! At any rate, I'm eager to meet you in Green Lawn, and I look forward to our lunch after the signing.

Wallis Wallace

"Wow!" said Ruth Rose. "First he says he's being followed, and then he winds up missing!"

Dink told Mavis about his letter from Wallis Wallace. "He said the only thing that would keep him from coming today was if he was kidnapped!"

"Oh, dear!" said Mavis. "I just don't understand. Why would anyone want to kidnap Wallis Wallace?"

"If he's the most famous mystery writer in the world, he must be rich, right?" Josh said. "Maybe someone kidnapped him for a ransom!"

Suddenly Josh grabbed Dink and spun him around, pointing toward the street. "Look! The cops are coming! They must have heard about the kidnapping!"

A police officer was walking toward them.

"Josh, that's just Officer Fallon,

Jimmy Fallon's grandfather," said Dink. "Jimmy came to get a book signed. I saw him inside the Book Nook."

"Maybe we should show Officer Fallon these letters," Ruth Rose suggested. "They could be clues if Wallis Wallace has really been kidnapped!"

"Who's been kidnapped?" asked Officer Fallon, who was now standing near them. "Not my grandson, I hope," he added, grinning.

Dink showed Officer Fallon the two letters. "We think Wallis Wallace might have been kidnapped," he said. "He promised he'd come to sign books, but he isn't here."

Officer Fallon read Mavis's letter first, then Dink's. He scratched his chin, then handed the letters back.

"The letters do sound a bit suspicious," he said. "But it's more likely that Mr. Wallace just missed his flight."

Jimmy Fallon ran out of the Book Nook, waving a Wallis Wallace book at his grandfather. "Grampa, he never came! Can we go for ice cream anyway?"

Officer Fallon put a big hand on Jimmy's head. "In a minute, son." To Dink he said, "I wouldn't worry. Mr. Wallace will turn up. Call me tomorrow if there's no news, okay?"

They watched Jimmy and his grandfather walk away.

Dink handed Mavis's letter back to her. He folded his and slid it into his pocket. Crazy thoughts were bouncing around in his head. *What if Wallis Wallace really has been kidnapped? It happened because I invited him to Green Lawn. I'm practically an accomplice!*

"I don't want to wait till tomorrow," he said finally. "I say we start looking for Wallis Wallace now!"

"Where do we start?" Ruth Rose asked.

Dink jerked his thumb over his shoulder. "Right here at the Book Nook."

"Excuse me," Mavis Green said shyly. "May I come along, too?"

"Sure," Dink said. He marched back inside the Book Nook, with the others following.

Mr. Paskey was putting the Wallis Wallace books back on a shelf. He looked even more nervous than before.

"Excuse me, Mr. Paskey," Dink said. "Have you heard from Wallis Wallace?"

Mr. Paskey's hand shot up to his bow tie. "No, Dink, not a word."

"We think he was kidnapped!" Josh said.

Mr. Paskey swallowed, making his bow tie wiggle. "Now, Joshua, let's not jump to conclusions. I'm sure there's a rational explanation for his absence."

Dink told Mr. Paskey about the two letters. "I'm really worried, Mr. Paskey. Where could he be?"

Mr. Paskey took out a handkerchief and wiped his face. "I have no idea." He removed a paper from his desk and handed it to Dink. "All I have is his itinerary."

The others looked over Dink's shoulder as he read:

Itinerary for Wallis Wallace:

1. Arrive at Bradley Airport at
   7:00 P.M., Friday, July 15,
   New England Airlines, Flight 3132.

2. Meet driver from Lawrence
   Taxi Service.

3. Drive to Shangri-La Hotel.

4. Sign books at Book Nook at 11:00 A.M.,
   Saturday, July 16.

5. Lunch, then back to airport for
   4:30 P.M. flight.

"Can I keep this?" Dink asked Mr. Paskey.

Mr. Paskey blinked. "Well, I guess that'll be all right. But why do you need the itinerary?"

Dink picked up a marker and drew circles around the words AIRPORT, TAXI, HOTEL, and BOOK NOOK.

"This is like a trail. It leads from the airport last night to the Book Nook today," Dink said. "Somewhere along this trail, Wallis Wallace disappeared."

Dink stared at the itinerary. "And we're going to find him!"

Chapter
4

Mr. Paskey shooed them out of the Book Nook and locked the front door. "I have to eat lunch," he said. He scurried down Main Street.

"Come on," Dink said. "There's a phone in Ellie's Diner."

"Good, we can eat while you're calling..." Josh stopped. "Who are you calling?"

"The airport," Dink said, "to see if Wallis Wallace was on that seven o'clock flight last night."

They walked into Ellie's Diner just

as Jimmy Fallon and his grandfather came out. Jimmy was working on a triple-decker chocolate cone.

Ellie stood behind the counter. As usual, her apron was smeared with ketchup, mustard, chocolate, and a lot of stuff Dink didn't recognize.

Ellie smiled. "Hi, Dink. Butter crunch, right?"

Dink shook his head. "No, thanks, Ellie. I came to use the phone."

"Excuse me, but would it be all right if I bought you each a cone?" Mavis Green asked. "I was going to buy lunch for Mr. Wallace anyway."

"Gee, thanks," Josh said. "I'll have a scoop of mint chip and a scoop of pistachio."

"Oh, you like green ice cream, too," Mavis said. She smiled shyly. "I'll have the same, please."

"I like pink ice cream," Ruth Rose

said. "I'll have a strawberry cone, please. One scoop."

"How about you, Dink?" Mavis asked.

"I'm not hungry, thanks," he said. "But you guys go ahead. I'm going to call the airport."

Dink felt guilty. If he hadn't invited Wallis Wallace to Green Lawn, his favorite author would be safe at home in his castle in Maine.

But Dink couldn't help feeling excited too. He felt like a detective from one of Wallis Wallace's books!

Dink stepped into the phone booth, looked up the number for New England Airlines, and called. When a voice came on, he asked if Wallis Wallace had been aboard Flight 3132 last night.

"He was? Did it land at seven o'clock?" Dink asked. "Thanks a lot!"

He rushed out of the phone booth. "Hey, guys, they told me Wallis Wallace was on the plane—and it landed right on time!"

"So he didn't miss his flight," Ruth Rose said through strawberry-pink lips.

"That's right!" Dink pulled out the itinerary. He drew a line through AIR-PORT.

"This is so exciting!" Ruth Rose said.

"Now what?" Josh asked, working on his double-dipper.

Dink pointed to his next circle on the itinerary. "Now we need to find out if a taxi picked him up," he said.

"Lawrence Taxi is over by the river," Ruth Rose said.

Dink looked at Mavis. "Would you like to come with us? We can walk there in five minutes."

Mavis Green wiped her lips carefully with a napkin. "I'd love to come," she said in her soft voice.

They left Ellie's Diner, walked left on Bridge Lane, then headed down Woodview Road toward the river.

"Mr. Paskey looked pretty upset, didn't he?" Josh said, crunching the last of his cone. His chin was green.

"Wouldn't you be upset if you had a bunch of customers at your store waiting to meet a famous author and he didn't show up?" Ruth Rose asked.

"Yeah, but he was sweating buckets," Josh said. "I wonder if Mr. Paskey kidnapped Wallis Wallace."

"Josh, get real! Why would Mr.

Paskey kidnap an author?" asked Ruth Rose. "He sells tons of Wallis Wallace's books!"

"I don't think Mr. Paskey is the kidnapper," Dink said. "But in a way, Josh is right. Detectives should consider everyone a suspect, just the way they do in Wallis Wallace's books."

At River Road, they turned left. Two minutes later, Dink pushed open the door of the Lawrence Taxi Service office. He asked the man behind the counter if one of their drivers had met Flight 3132 at Bradley Airport the previous night.

The man ran his finger down a list on a clipboard. "That would be Maureen Higgins. She's out back eating her lunch," he said, pointing over his shoulder. "Walk straight through."

They cut through the building to a grassy area in back. Through the trees,

Dink could see the Indian River. The sun reflected off the water like bright coins.

A woman was sitting at a picnic table eating a sandwich and filling in a crossword puzzle.

"Excuse me, are you Maureen Higgins?" Dink asked.

The woman shook her head without looking up. "Nope, I'm Marilyn Monroe."

The woman wrote in another letter. Then she looked up. She had the merriest blue eyes Dink had ever seen.

"Yeah, cutie pie, I'm Maureen." She pointed her sandwich at Dink. "And who might you be?"

"I'm Dink Duncan," he said. "These are my friends Josh, Ruth Rose, and Mavis."

"We wondered if you could help us," Ruth Rose said.

Maureen stared at them. "How?"

"Did you pick up a man named Wallis Wallace at the airport last night?" Dink asked.

Maureen squinted one of her blue eyes. "Why do you want to know?"

"Because he's missing!" said Josh.

"Well, I sure ain't got him!" Maureen took a bite out of her sandwich. Mayonnaise oozed onto her fingers.

"I know. I mean, we didn't think you had him," Dink said. "But did you pick him up?"

Maureen nodded, swallowing. "Sure I picked him up. Seven o'clock sharp, I was there with my sign saying WALLACE. The guy spots me, trots over, I take him out to my taxi. He climbs in, carrying a small suitcase. Kinda spooky guy. Dressed in a hat, long raincoat, sunglasses. Sunglasses at night! Doesn't speak a word, just sits. Spooky!"

"Did you take him to the Shangri-la Hotel?" Dink asked.

"Yep. Those were my orders. Guy didn't have to give directions, but it woulda been nice if he'd said something. Pass the time, you know? Lotta people, they chat just to act friendly. Not this one. Quiet as a mouse in the back seat."

Maureen wiped mayonnaise from her fingers and lips. "Who is this Wallace fella, anyway?"

"He's a famous writer!" Ruth Rose said.

Maureen's mouth fell open. "You mean I had a celebrity in my cab and never even knew it?"

"What happened when you got to the hotel?" Josh asked.

Maureen stood up and tossed her napkin into the trash. "I get out of my side, then I open his door. He hops out,

hands me a twenty. Last I seen, he's scooting into the lobby."

Dink pulled out the itinerary. He crossed out TAXI with a thick black line. Then he drew a question mark next to HOTEL.

"Thanks a lot, Miss Higgins," he said. "Come on, guys, I have a feeling we're getting closer to finding Wallis Wallace."

Maureen put her hand on Dink's arm. "I just thought of something," she said. "When he handed me my fare, this Wallace fella was smiling."

Dink stared at Maureen. "Smiling?"

She nodded. "Yep. Had a silly grin on his face. Like he knew some big secret or something."

Chapter 5

Back on Main Street, Dink adjusted his backpack and led the way to the Shangri-la Hotel.

"Maureen Higgins said she dropped him off at the hotel last night," he told the others, "so that's our next stop."

"What if she didn't?" Josh said, catching up to Dink.

"What do you mean?"

"I mean maybe Maureen Higgins wasn't telling the truth. Maybe *she* kidnapped him!"

"And she's hiding him in her lunch-

box!" Ruth Rose said.

"Very funny, Ruth Rose," Josh said. "Maureen Higgins said she drove Wallis Wallace to the hotel. But what if she drove him somewhere else?"

"You could be right," Dink said. "That's why we're going to the hotel."

With Dink in the lead, the four approached the check-in counter in the hotel lobby.

"Excuse me," Dink said to the man behind the counter.

"May we help you?" He was the saddest-looking man Dink had ever seen. He had thin black hair and droopy eyebrows. His skinny mustache looked like a sleeping centipede. A name tag on his suit coat said MR. LINKLETTER.

"We're looking for someone."

Mr. Linkletter stared at Dink.

"He's supposed to be staying in this hotel," Josh said.

The man twitched his mustache at Josh.

"His name is Wallis Wallace," Dink explained. "Can you tell us if he checked in last night?"

Mr. Linkletter patted his mustache. "Young sir, if we had such a guest, we wouldn't give out any information. We have *rules* at the Shangri-la," he added in a deep, sad voice.

"But he's missing!" Ruth Rose said. "He was supposed to be at the Book Nook this morning and he never showed up!"

Dink pulled out the itinerary. "See, he was coming here from the airport. The taxi driver said she saw him walk into this lobby."

"And he's famous!" Ruth Rose said. She placed her book on the counter in front of Mr. Linkletter. "He wrote this!"

Sighing, Mr. Linkletter looked down

at Ruth Rose. "We are quite aware of who Mr. Wallace is, young miss."

Mr. Linkletter turned his sad eyes back on Dink. He flipped through the hotel register, glanced at it, then quickly shut the book. "Yes, Mr. Wallace checked in," he said. "He arrived at 8:05."

"He did? What happened after that?" Dink asked.

Mr. Linkletter pointed toward a bank of elevators. "He went to his room. We offered to have his suitcase carried, but he preferred to do it himself."

"Have you seen Mr. Wallace yet today?" Mavis asked.

"No, madam, I haven't seen him. Mr. Wallace is still in his room."

Still in his room!

Suddenly Dink felt relieved. He felt a little foolish, too. Wallis Wallace hadn't been kidnapped after all. He was probably in his room right now!

"Can you call him?" Dink asked.

Mr. Linkletter tapped his fingers on the closed hotel register. He patted his mustache and squinted his eyes at Dink.

"Please?" Dink said. "We just want to make sure he's okay."

Finally Mr. Linkletter turned around. He stepped a few feet away and picked up a red telephone.

As soon as his back was turned, Josh grabbed the hotel register. He quickly found yesterday's page. Dink and the others crowded around Josh for a peek.

Dink immediately recognized Wallis Wallace's signature, scrawled in big loopy letters. He had checked in to Room 303 at five after eight last night.

Dink pulled out his letter from Wallis Wallace and compared the two

signatures. They were exactly the same.

Josh dug his elbow into Dink's side. "Look!" he whispered.

Josh was pointing at the next line in the register. ROOM 302 had been printed there. Check-in time was 8:15.

"Someone else checked in right after

Wallis Wallace!" Ruth Rose whispered.

"But the signature is all smudged," Dink said. "I can't read the name."

When Mr. Linkletter hung up the phone, Josh shoved the register away.

As Mr. Linkletter turned back around, Dink shut the register. He looked up innocently. "Is he in his room?" Dink asked.

"I don't know." Mr. Linkletter tapped his fingers on his mustache. "There was no answer."

Dink's stomach dropped. His mind raced.

If Wallis Wallace had checked into his room last night, why hadn't he shown up at the Book Nook today?

And why wasn't he answering his phone?

Maybe Wallis Wallace had been kidnapped after all!

Chapter 6

Dink stared at Mr. Linkletter. "No answer? Are you sure?"

Mr. Linkletter nodded. He looked puzzled. "Perhaps he's resting and doesn't want to be disturbed."

"Can we go up and see?" Ruth Rose smiled sweetly at Mr. Linkletter. "Then we'd know for sure."

Mr. Linkletter shook his head. "We cannot disturb our guests, young miss. We have *rules* at the Shangri-la. Now good day, and thank you."

Ruth Rose opened her mouth. "But, Mis—"

"Good day," Mr. Linkletter said firmly again.

Dink and the others walked toward the door.

"Something smells fishy," muttered Dink.

"Yeah," Josh said, "and I think it's that Linkletter guy. See how he tried to hide the register? Then he turned his back. Maybe he didn't even call Room 303. Maybe he was warning his partners in crime!"

"What are you suggesting, Josh?" Mavis asked.

"Maybe Mr. Linkletter is the kidnapper," Josh said. "He was the last one to see Wallis Wallace."

A man wearing a red cap tapped Dink on the shoulder. "Excuse me, but I overheard you talking to my boss, Mr.

Linkletter. Maybe I can help you find Wallis Wallace. My kids love his books."

"Great!" Dink said. "Can you get us into his room?"

The man shook his head. "No, but I know the maid who cleaned the third-floor rooms this morning. Maybe she noticed something."

With his back to Mr. Linkletter, the man scribbled a few words on a pad and handed the page to Dink. "Good luck!" the man whispered, and hurried away.

"What'd he write?" Josh asked.

"Outside," Dink said.

They all shoved through the revolving door. In front of the hotel, Dink looked at the piece of paper. "The maid's name is Olivia Nugent. She lives at the Acorn Apartments, Number Four."

"Livvy Nugent? I know her!" Ruth Rose said. "She used to be my baby-sitter."

"The Acorn is right around the corner on Oak Street," Dink said. "Let's go!"

Soon all four were standing in front of Livvy Nugent's door. She answered it with a baby in her arms. Another little kid held on to her leg and stared at Dink and the others. He had peanut butter all over his face and in his hair.

"Hi," the boy's mother said. "I'm not buying any cookies and I already get the *Green Lawn Gazette.*" She was wearing a man's blue shirt and jeans. Her brown hair stuck out from under a Yankees baseball cap.

"Livvy, it's me!" Ruth Rose said.

Olivia stared at Ruth Rose, then broke into a grin.

"Ruth Rose, you're so big! What are

you up to these days?"

"A man at the hotel gave us your name."

"What man?"

"He was sort of old, wearing a red cap," Dink said.

Livvy chuckled. "Freddy old? He's only thirty! So why did he send you to see me?"

"He told us you cleaned the rooms on the third floor this morning," Dink said. "Did you clean Room 303?"

Livvy Nugent shifted the baby to her other arm. "Randy, please stop pulling on Mommy's leg. Why don't you go finish your lunch?" Randy ran back into the apartment.

"No," Livvy told Dink. "Nobody slept in that room. The bed was still made this morning. The towels were still clean and dry. I remember because there were two rooms in a row that I

didn't have to clean—303 and 302. Room 302 had a Do Not Disturb sign hanging on the doorknob. So I came home early, paid off the baby-sitter, and made our lunches."

"But Mr. Linkletter told us Wallis

Wallace checked into Room 303 last night," Ruth Rose said.

"Not *the* Wallis Wallace? The mystery writer? My kid sister *devours* his books!"

Dink nodded. "He was supposed to sign books at the Book Nook this morning. But he never showed up!"

"We even saw his signature on the hotel register," Ruth Rose said.

"Well, Wallis Wallace might have signed in, but he never slept in that room." Livvy grinned. "Unless he's a ghost."

"I wonder if Mr. Linkletter could have made a mistake about the room number," Mavis suggested quietly.

Livvy smiled at Mavis. "You must not be from around here. Mr. Linkletter *never* makes mistakes."

"So Wallis Wallace signed in, but he didn't sleep in his room," said Dink.

"That means..."

"Someone must have kidnapped him before he went to bed!" Josh said.

Livvy's eyes bugged. "Kidnapped! Geez, Mr. Linkletter will have a fit." She imitated his voice. "We have *rules* about kidnappings at the Shangri-la!"

Everyone except Dink laughed. All he could think about was Wallis Wallace, his favorite author, kidnapped.

Suddenly a crash came from inside the apartment. "Oops, gotta run," Livvy said. "Randy is playing bulldozer with his baby sister's stroller again. I hope you find Wallis Wallace. My kid sister will die if he doesn't write another book!"

They walked slowly back to Main Street. Dink felt as though his brain was spinning around inside his head.

Now he felt certain that Wallis Wallace had been kidnapped.

But who did it? And when?

And where was Wallis Wallace being kept?

"Guys, I'm feeling confused," he said. "Can we just sit somewhere and go over the facts again?"

"Good idea," Josh said. "I always think better when I'm eating."

"I'm feeling a bit peckish, too," Mavis said. "I need a quiet cup of tea and a sandwich. Should we meet again after lunch?"

Ruth Rose looked at her watch. "Let's meet at two o'clock."

"Where?" Josh asked.

"Back at the hotel." Dink peered through the door glass at Mr. Linkletter.

"Unless Maureen Higgins and Mr. Linkletter are *both* lying," he said, "Wallis Wallace walked into the Shangri-la last night—and never came out."

Chapter 7

Dink, Josh, and Ruth Rose left Mavis at Ellie's Diner, then headed for Dink's house. Dink made tuna sandwiches and lemonade. Ruth Rose brought a bag of potato chips and some raisin cookies from her house next door.

They ate at the picnic table in Dink's backyard. Dink took a bite of his sandwich. After he swallowed, he said, "Let's go over what we know."

He moved his lemonade glass to the middle of the table. "My glass is the airport," he said. "We know Wallis Wallace landed."

"How do we *know* he did?" Josh asked.

"The airport told me the plane landed, Josh."

"And Maureen Higgins said she picked him up," Ruth Rose added.

"Okay, so your glass is the airport," Josh said. "Keep going, Dink."

Dink slid his sandwich plate over next to his glass. "My plate is Maureen's taxi." He put a cookie on the plate. "The cookie is Wallis Wallace getting into the taxi."

Dink slid the plate over to the opened potato chip bag. "This bag is the hotel." He walked the Wallis Wallace cookie from the plate into the bag.

Dink looked at Josh and Ruth Rose. "But what happened to Wallis Wallace after he walked into the lobby?"

"I'll tell you what happened," Josh said. He lined up four cookies in a row. "This little cookie is Mr. Paskey. These three are Maureen, Mr. Linkletter, and Olivia Nugent."

Josh looked up and waggled his eyebrows. "I think these four cookies planned the kidnapping *together!*"

Ruth Rose laughed. "Josh, Mr. Paskey and Livvy Nugent are friends of ours. Do you really think they planned this big kidnapping? And can you see Mr. Linkletter and my baby-sitter pulling off a kidnapping together?"

Josh ate a potato chip. "Well, maybe not. But *someone* kidnapped the guy!"

"Our trail led us to the hotel, and then it ended," Dink said. "What I want to know is, if Wallis Wallace isn't in his room, where is he?"

Dink nibbled on a cookie thoughtfully. "I'm getting a headache trying to sort it all out."

Ruth Rose dug in Dink's backpack and brought out three Wallis Wallace books. "I have an idea." She handed books to Dink and Josh and kept one.

"What're these for?" Dink asked.

"Josh made me think of something Wallis Wallace wrote in *The Mystery in the Museum*," Ruth Rose said. "He said the more you know about the victim, the easier it is to figure out who did the crime."

She turned to the back cover of her book. "So let's try to find out more about our victim. Listen to this." She started reading out loud. "'When not writing, the author likes to work in the garden. Naturally, Wallis Wallace's favorite color is green.'"

"Fine," said Josh, "but how does knowing his favorite color help us find him, Ruth Rose?"

"I don't know, but maybe if we read more about him, we'll discover some clues," Ruth Rose said. "What does it say on the back of your book?"

Josh flipped the book over and began

reading. "'Wallis Wallace lives in a castle called Moose Manor.'" He looked up. "We already knew he lived in a castle. I don't see any clues yet, you guys."

Ruth Rose stared at Josh. "You know, something is bugging me, but I can't figure out what it is. Something someone said today, maybe." She shook her head. "Anyway, read yours, Dink."

Dink read from the back cover of his book. "'Wallis Wallace gives money from writing books to help preserve the wild animals that live in Maine.'"

"Okay, he gives money away to save animals, lives in a castle, and grows a bunch of green stuff," Josh said, counting on his fingers. "Still no clues."

Josh took another cookie. "But I just thought of something." He began slowly munching on the cookie.

Dink raised his eyebrows. "Are you going to tell us, Josh?"

"Well, I was thinking about Room 302. Remember, someone signed the register right after Wallis Wallace checked into Room 303? And the signature was all smudged? And then Olivia Nugent—"

"—told us that Room 302 had a Do Not Disturb sign on it!" Ruth Rose interrupted. "Livvy never went into that room at all!"

Just then Dink's mother drove up the driveway. She got out of the car, waved, and started walking toward the picnic table.

"Oh, no!" Dink said. "If Mom finds out I'm trying to find a kidnapper, she won't let me out of the house! Don't say anything, okay?"

"Can't I even say hi?" Josh asked.

Dink threw a potato chip at Josh. "Say hi, then shut up about you-know-what!"

"Hi, Mrs. Duncan!" Josh said, sliding a look at Dink.

"Hi, kids. How was the book signing? Tell me all about Wallis Wallace, Dink. Is he as wonderful as you expected?"

Dink stared at his mother. He didn't want to lie. But if he told her the truth, she wouldn't let him keep looking for Wallis Wallace. And Dink had a sudden feeling that they were very close to finding him.

We can't stop now! he thought. He looked at his mother and grinned stupidly.

"Dink? Honey? Why is your mouth open?"

He closed his mouth. *Think, Dink!* he ordered himself.

Suddenly Josh knocked over his lemonade glass. The sticky cold liquid spilled into Dink's lap.

Dink let out a yowl and jumped up.

"Gee, sorry!" said Josh.

"Paper towels to the rescue!" Dink's mother ran toward the house.

"Good thinking, Josh," Dink said, wiping at his wet jeans. "But did you have to spill it on *me?* You had the whole yard!"

Josh grinned. "Some people are never satisfied. I got you out of hot water, didn't I?"

"Right into cold lemonade," Ruth Rose said.

Dink blotted his jeans with a handful of paper napkins. "Come on. Let's go meet Mavis before my mom comes back. There's something weird happening on the third floor of the Shangri-la!"

Chapter 8

Dink's jeans were nearly dry by the time they reached the hotel. Mavis was waiting out front.

"How was your lunch?" she asked timidly.

"Fine, thanks," Dink said. "We talked it over, and we think there's something fishy going on on the third floor of this hotel."

Suddenly Mavis began coughing. She held up her scarf in front of her mouth.

Dink noticed that the letters on the

scarf were tiny M's. "Are you okay?" he asked.

"Should I run in and get you some water?" asked Josh.

Mavis took off her glasses and shook her head. "No, I'm fine, thank you. Dear me, I don't know what happened! Now, what were you saying about the third floor?"

"We think Wallis Wallace may be up there," Ruth Rose said. She reminded Mavis about the smudged signature for Room 302 and the Do Not Disturb sign on the door.

Mavis replaced her eyeglasses. "Mercy! What do you think we should do?"

"Follow me!" Dink said. For the second time, they all trooped into the hotel lobby.

Mr. Linkletter watched them from behind the counter.

"Hi," Dink said. "Remember us?"

"Vividly," Mr. Linkletter said.

"Wallis Wallace checked into Room 303, right?"

"That is correct," said Mr. Linkletter.

"Well, we talked to the maid who cleaned that room," Dink went on. "She told us no one slept in it."

"You spoke to Olivia Nugent? When? How?"

"We have our ways," Josh said.

"So," Dink went on, "we think Wallis Wallace disappeared right here in this hotel."

"And Wallis Wallace is a *very* famous writer," Ruth Rose reminded Mr. Linkletter. "Millions of kids are waiting to read his next book," she added sweetly.

Mr. Linkletter's sad eyes grew large. He swallowed and his Adam's apple bobbed up and down. He rubbed his

forehead as though he had a headache.

Then Dink told Mr. Linkletter about Room 302. "Miss Nugent said there was a Do Not Disturb sign on the door."

Ruth Rose pointed to the register. "See? The signature is all smudged!"

"We think the kidnappers are hiding Wallis Wallace in that room!" Josh said.

At the word "kidnappers," Mr. Linkletter closed his eyes. He opened a drawer, took out a bottle of headache pills, and put one on his tongue.

"Just to be on the safe side, perhaps we should check both rooms, Mr. Linkletter," Mavis said quietly.

"It'll just take a minute," Dink said.

Mr. Linkletter let out a big sigh. "Very well, but this is most unusual. Things run very smoothly at the Shangrila."

They all got into the elevator. No one spoke. Dink watched Mr. Linkletter jiggling his bunch of keys. Mr. Linkletter kept his eyes on the little arrow telling them which floor they were on.

The elevator door opened on the third floor. Mr. Linkletter unlocked Room 303. "Most unusual," he muttered.

The room was empty and spotlessly clean. "Strange, very strange," Mr. Linkletter said.

They moved to Room 302, where a Do Not Disturb sign still hung on the doorknob.

Mr. Linkletter knocked. They all leaned toward the door.

"Listen, I hear a voice!" Josh said.

"What's it saying?" Ruth Rose asked.

Then they all heard it.

The voice was muffled, but it was definitely yelling, "HELP!"

Chapter 9

Mr. Linkletter unlocked the door and shoved it open.

A man with curly blond hair stared back at them. He was sitting in a chair with his feet tied in front of him. His arms were tied behind his back. A towel was wrapped around his mouth.

"Oh, my goodness!" Mr. Linkletter cried.

Everyone rushed into the room.

Dink ran behind the chair to untie the man's hands while Josh untied his

feet.

Mavis unwrapped the towel from around his face.

"Thank goodness you got here!" the man said. "I'm Wallis Wallace. Someone knocked on my door last night. A voice said he was from room service. When I opened the door, two men dragged me in here and tied me up."

He looked at Dink. "You're Dink Duncan! I recognize you from the picture you sent. How did you find me?"

"We followed your itinerary," Dink said. He showed Mr. Wallace the sheet of paper. "We got it from Mr. Paskey and used it as a trail. The trail led us to this room!"

"I'm so sorry I missed the book signing," Wallis Wallace said. "As you can see, I was a bit tied up."

He smiled. Then he rubbed his jaw. "My mouth is sore from that towel. I

can't believe I was kidnapped! And I can't wait to get back to my safe little cottage in Maine."

"Can you describe the two guys who kidnapped you?" Dink asked. "We should tell Officer Fallon so he can try to find them."

Wallis Wallace stared at Dink. "The two guys? Oh...well, um, I don't think I'll—"

"HEY!" Ruth Rose suddenly yelled.

Everyone looked at her.

"What's the matter?" asked Dink. "You look funny, Ruth Rose."

Ruth Rose was staring at the red scarf draped around Mavis's neck. She pointed at the man who'd been tied up. "You're not Wallis Wallace!"

Then she looked at Mavis Green. "*You* are," she said quietly.

Chapter 10

"Ruth Rose, what are you talking about?" Josh said.

Dink didn't know what to think, except that he was getting a headache.

"What makes you think *I'm* Wallis Wallace?" Mavis asked.

Ruth Rose walked over to Mavis. "May I borrow your scarf?" she said.

Ruth Rose held the scarf up so everyone could see it. "When I first saw this scarf, I thought these little black letters were M's," she said. "M for Mavis."

She looked at Mavis Green. "But they're not M's, are they?"

She turned the scarf completely upside down. "What do they look like now?"

Dink stepped closer. "They're little W's now!"

"Right. Double-U, double-U for *Wallis Wallace!*" Ruth Rose pointed at the man. "You just said you live in a little cottage. But Wallis Wallace lives in a big *castle* in Maine. It says so on the cover of *The Silent Swamp.*"

Ruth Rose pointed at Mavis's book bag. "Seeing your bag again made me remember something I thought of today. Josh read that your castle was called Moose Manor. There's a picture of a moose on the side of your bag."

Ruth Rose handed the scarf back to Mavis. "And we read that Wallis Wallace's favorite color is green. You like green ice cream, and you chose Mavis Green for your fake name."

Everyone was staring at Ruth Rose, except for the man they had untied. He started laughing.

"The cat's out of the bag now, sis," he said.

Then Mavis laughed and gave Ruth Rose a hug.

"Yes, Ruth Rose," Mavis said. "I really *am* Wallis Wallace." She put her hand on the man's shoulder. "And this is my brother, Walker Wallace. We've been planning my 'kidnapping' for weeks!"

Dink stared at Mavis, or whoever she was. "You mean Wallis Wallace is a woman?" he said.

"Yes, Dink, I'm a woman, and I'm definitely Wallis Wallace." She winked at him. "Honest!"

Mavis, the real Wallis Wallace, sat on the bed. She took off her glasses and pulled the barrettes out of her hair. She shook her hair until it puffed out in a mass of wild curls.

"Thank goodness I can be myself now!" she said. "All day I've had to act like timid Mavis Green. I can't wait to get out of this fuddy-duddy dress and into my jeans again!"

She kicked off her shoes and wiggled her toes in the air. "Boy, does that feel good!"

Dink blinked and shook his head. Mavis Green was really Wallis Wallace? He couldn't believe it. "But why did you pretend to be kidnapped?" he asked.

The real Wallis Wallace grinned at the kids' surprised faces. "I owe you an explanation," she said.

"My new book is about a children's mystery writer who gets kidnapped. In my book, some children rescue the

writer. I wanted to find out how *real* kids might solve the mystery," she explained.

She smiled at Dink. "Then your letter came, inviting me to Green Lawn. That's what gave me the idea to fake my own kidnapping. I'd become Mavis Green and watch what happened."

"Oh, yeah!" Dink said. "In your let-

ter, you said you were doing some research in Connecticut."

She nodded. "Yes, and I mentioned the word 'kidnap' in the letter to get you thinking along those lines." She smiled at the three kids. "I thought I'd have to give you more clues, but you solved the mystery all by yourselves!"

Dink laughed. "You recognized me in

the bookstore from my picture," he said. "And you didn't send *me* a picture so I wouldn't recognize *you!*"

"Then my nutty sister dragged *me* into her plan," Walker Wallace said. "I should be home checking my lobster pots."

"While you were eating lunch, Walker and I ate ours up here," Wallis said. "Then, just before two o'clock, I tied him in the chair and ran downstairs to meet you out front as Mavis."

Wallis Wallace threw back her head and laughed. "Do you remember downstairs when Dink said there was something fishy on the third floor?"

She got up and stood next to her brother. "Well, I'm always teasing Walker about smelling fishy from handling his lobster bait. So when you said something was *fishy* in the hotel, I had to pretend to cough so you wouldn't

know I was really laughing!"

"Boy, did you have us fooled," Dink said.

Wallis Wallace grinned. "Mr. Paskey was in on it. I had to tell him the truth. As you saw this morning at the Book Nook, my little scheme made him very nervous. I've promised him I'll come back and do a real book signing soon. But I'll be in disguise, so be prepared for anything!"

Dink shook his head. "I was so disappointed because I couldn't meet my favorite author this morning," he said. "And I've been with you all day and didn't even know it!"

She looked at Dink. "I'm so sorry I tricked you. Will you forgive me?"

Dink blushed. "Sure."

"I have a question," Josh said. "Where did you really sleep last night?"

"Right here in Room 302. A few

weeks ago, I telephoned to reserve two rooms next to each other. Last night, I checked into Room 303 as Wallis Wallace, the man. Up in Room 303, I took off the hat and coat and sunglasses. Then I sneaked back down to the lobby wearing a blond wig. I checked in again, this time into Room 302."

"Did you smudge the signature?" Ruth Rose asked.

"Oh, you noticed that!" Wallis said. "I'm so used to signing my real name in books, I started to write *Wallis*. So I 'accidentally' smudged it."

"I have a question, Mavis, I mean Miss Wallace...what should we call you?" Dink asked.

"My friends call me Wallis," she said.

"Well, the taxi driver told us you were smiling in the taxi. What were you smiling about?"

Wallis Wallace was smiling now.

"Oh, about a lot of things. First, I was wearing a man's disguise, and that made me feel pretty silly. And I knew I was going to meet you, one of my biggest fans. And I was happy because I knew whatever happened, the next day would be fun!"

"I sure had fun," Josh said, grinning. "Poor Mr. Paskey, having to lie to everyone with a straight face!"

"Boy, did I have a hard time pretending to be Mavis all day," Wallis said. "But my plan worked. I met three brilliant detectives. You helped me to see how real kids would investigate a kidnapping. Now I can go back to Maine and finish my book."

"How come your book jackets never say that you're a woman?" Ruth Rose asked.

Wallis Wallace smiled. "Because of my name, most people assume that I'm a man," she explained. "I let them think that so I can do my research easier. I've learned that people clam up if they know I'm Wallis Wallace. So out in public I pretend I'm Mavis Green, just a regular person, not a mystery writer."

"I get it!" Dink said. "You don't have your picture on your books so people can't recognize you."

"Right. And I hope you'll keep my secret."

"We will. Right, guys?" Ruth Rose said.

"Thank you! Any more questions?" Wallis asked.

"Yeah," Walker said, giving his sister a look. "When do we leave? I've got lobsters waiting for me."

"I have a question, too," Dink said. "Will you send me your picture now?"

"Yes, but I'll do better than that," Wallis said. "I'll dedicate my next book

to my three new friends!"

Dink, Josh, and Ruth Rose did a triple high five.

"Excuse me," Mr. Linkletter said from the door where he had been standing.

They all looked at him.

"It's nearly checkout time."

Everyone laughed.

Mr. Linkletter smiled, but just a little.

HAVE YOU READ ALL THE BOOKS IN THE

A to Z Mysteries®

SERIES?

Help Dink, Josh, and Ruth Rose . . .

...solve
mysteries
from A to Z!

Collect clues with
Dink, Josh, and Ruth Rose
in their next exciting
adventure!

THE
BALD
BANDIT

The detective looked at the three friends.

"Tell you what," he said. "If you find the kid who filmed the robber, get the video. There'll be a nice reward if you hand it over."

"How much?" Josh asked.

"How about one hundred dollars for each of you?"

"A HUNDRED BUCKS?" screamed Ruth Rose.

The detective pulled out a small pad and a pencil. He wrote something and ripped off the page.

"Here's my phone number. Call me if you get that video."

Dink closed the door behind Detective Reddy. He grinned at Josh and Ruth Rose. "A hundred bucks each! We're rich!"